the jar menagerie

monica babich
c.s. fritz

For more information visit:
www.beingintuit.com/the-jar-menagerie

Illustrations by C.S. Fritz
Editing and formatting by Albatross Book Co.
www.albatrossbookco.com

ISBN (hardback): 978-0-578-95967-2

For Eli

A boy took a jar from the top, wide shelf.
He leapt down to earth, feeling proud himself.
He fashioned a lid from a hole-punched sheet,
With string tied around it, so terribly neat.

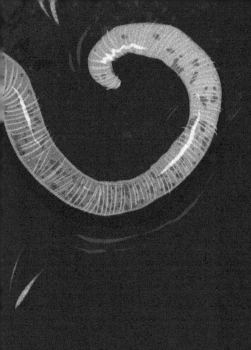

Then outside he strolled with his jar in tow
To find himself pets in the ground below.
Where under a rock he found five, fat worms.
He squealed with delight and beheld their squirms.

Into the jar went the whole wriggly pack.
On went the lid, and the boy raced right back.
Replacing the jar on his desk's top shelf,
He reached for another one by himself.

Then filling it up, 'til almost the brim,
With just enough water for someone's swim;
He left for the creek and raced like a dog,
With dreams of collecting a pollywog.

He stumbled upon one and swooped up quick,
A giant green tadpole whose tail flick-kicked.
So on went the lid, and the boy smiled big.
And back to the house he skipped with a jig.

Down went a third jar, and out ran the boy,
One's own private zoo's the ultimate toy!
And out in the garden, right next to a slug,
He zoomed his eyes onto a small ladybug.

His search not yet over, oh no siree,
How could he complete his menagerie?
Perhaps with a fish? Or a frog, or three?
A cricket or spider, or just one flea?

So into the shed he went to find jars,
When he tripped on himself, fell, and saw stars.
Then click went the latch of the old shed's door;
(The boy fell asleep on the cold, hard floor!)

A few hours passed, and the boy came-to.
He got to his feet, and thought, "What to do?!"
"Come HELP me!" he yelled, "I'm locked here inside!"
He pounded his fists, he screamed and he cried.

The darkness came over, his hunger - strong.
He started to wonder if he'd been wrong . . .
Those pets were not his - they're meant for outside.
Their freedom and life, of them he'd denied.

He pledged to himself, trapped there in that shed,
To stop keeping pets in jars and instead,
Make it his mission to find creatures' digs -
A puddle, a dirt pile or fresh green sprigs.

That night, about seven, the air was still.
He heard his mom shouting out,"Will, Will, WILL!?!"
His heart leapt a beat and his hopes did too.
"Ma-ma!" he screamed out, and then,"I hear you!"

When off popped the latch and into her hold
Went poor, tired William, who felt consoled.
The very next day, he awoke quite bright.
Reminded of all he'd said he'd put right.

He first homed the worms - he found them a stump;
The tadpole was ready for his high jump
Back into the pond and the warm waters -
The ladybug thrilled to see her daughters.

The now-empty jars he brought to the sink,
And then Will laid down to have a long think . . .
And that's when our boy hatched a great big plan
"To rescue as many more as I can!"

He needed to get to a big pet store -
He begged and he pleaded his parents more.
Then one hour later, they drove straight there.
He walked up the rows with pets everywhere.

Aisle three had the lizards and crickets too;
He filled up his arms with more than a few.
His pockets were lined with quarters galore;
Two dollars short, Daddy loaned him eight more.

With bagfuls of critters on either side,
He sat in the backseat, smile big and wide.
Those crickets were destined for something more.
He'd quite the surprise for them all in store.

So down by the creek he skipped with delight.
(Remember his pledge to make things all right?)
He opened the baggies and watched them flee;
For certain he heard them all shout, "Yippee!"

They scattered around and hopped out of sight;
They chirped and they jumped in grateful delight.
And William, you know, he felt just darn great!
He spread around news of their joyous fate!

And never again did he capture more,
Believing captivity's quite the bore.
"It's better for creatures to play out-wild,"
So says this young, happy-go-lucky child.

Fear not for your pets who can roam around,
But leave the poor souls who crawl on the ground,

Or fly in the sky, or live but a day,
'Cause creatures have feelings, too, by the way.

A life in a jar is not one at all -
(No matter if tiny or big or small.)
Will's parents, they fixed up that old shed's latch.
And Will leaves the bugs to the veggie patch.

The End.

CPSIA information can be obtained
at www.ICGtesting.com
Printed in the USA
BVHW020837171121
621777BV00008B/609